The BAT BOOK

Afraid of a BAT? What's Up With That?!

by Conrad J. Storad   Illustrated by Nate & Tristan Jensen

Dedications:

For a new generation of young readers:
Granddaughter Hadley Jane and my new grand nieces and nephews:
Kendall, Layne, Norah Gene, Carter, and Rockwell
--CJS

For all my friends and family in my old hometown
Austin, TX
--NPJ

For my classmates at Stephenson Elementary
--TBJ

Acknowledgements:

Special thanks to Micaela Jemison, communications manager for Bat Conservation International in Arlington, Virginia, and Dianne Odegard, education and public outreach manager for BCI in Austin, Texas. Your comments and suggestions for improving this book were very helpful. The updates for the "Facts to Drive You Batty" page will be much appreciated by young readers everywhere.

More critter books available online at bobolinkmedia.com

Text copyright © 2015 by Conrad J. Storad
Illustrations copyright © 2015 by Nathaniel P. Jensen

For further information, write to Bobolink Media, Inc., Fallbrook, CA
bobolink@roadrunner.com
www.bobolinkmedia.com

BOBOLINK MEDIA

The illustrations were rendered in watercolor on Arches paper. .
The type was set in Trebuchet MS, Bang Whack Pow, Arial Black
Composed in the United States of America
Graphic layout by Nate Jensen
Conrad Storad's photo by Linda F. Radke
Production supervision and coordination by Steve Coppock
Printed by Arizona Lithography, Tuscon, AZ, USA

First impression
Library of Congress Control Number:
International Standard Book Number: ISBN 978-1-891795-66-x

Bats are NOT scary!

Under a bridge in Texas lives a bat. In fact, more than a million bats live under that bridge. I am just one of them.
I am Little Boy Bat.
Keep it simple.
Just call me LB.

My name in human language is almost impossible to say. It would sound something like

Skreeexxzzyyzz,

if your ears could hear it at all. No worries. Conrad is a pretty good translator of bat talk. And Nate is a great artist. Together, they will make the squiggles and symbols and pictures on the pages of this book to help tell you my story.

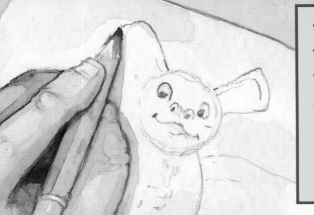

1

Right off the bat, errrr, I mean, the first thing I have to say is very, VERY important.

Are you ready to listen? Here it is: BATS ARE NOT SCARY!

Are you afraid of bats? If so, what's up with that?

We are so misunderstood.

Please, don't be afraid of bats.

Did you understand me? Once again. It's easy to remember:

Bats are NOT scary !

My mom and dad thought it was a great idea for me to write this book for you and other humans. I want to help you better understand bats like me. So keep reading.

We are mammals, just like you.

But bats are the only mammal that can fly.

Pretty cool, don't you think?

I am not bragging, but bats are some of the most important animals in the world. There are more than 1,300 different kinds of bats. Probably lots more than that.

Bats live in almost every habitat on Planet Earth. Well, not in the Arctic or in Antarctica. It's too dang cold in both of those places.

We live in caves,

under cliffs

and bridges

and the eaves of roofs.

Many of my forest cousins like to hang out in trees.

Bats like to live together. Our family group is called a colony. Some bat colonies include millions of bats.

Lots of bat colonies are quite famous. For example, I live under the Congress Avenue Bridge, in Austin, Texas, with with my family and more than a million cousins. Texas is home to many famous bat colonies. Bracken Cave is located just outside of San Antonio, Texas. That cave is home to the largest known bat colony on Earth. As many as 15 million bats live there. In the spring, it can be even more than that when the new pups are born.

Of course, there are other famous bat colonies. Many of my cousins live at Kartchner Caverns in Arizona. Carlsbad Caverns in New Mexico is home to a big colony of bats. Bats live in every state in America.

Bats come in all shapes and sizes.
Some of us are tiny. Others are quite large.

Bats have cool names, too.

There are Bulldog bats

and Hog-nosed bats,

Painted bats

and Mouse-tailed bats.

There are Flying foxes

and Thumbless bats.

Some have short **tails**.

Others have **long** tails.

Some have **long** tongues

and others have **long** noses.

There are **big** brown bats

and little brown bats.

And yes, there are Vampire bats.

5

Me, I'm a Mexican free-tailed bat.

Before you turn the page...

Bats are NOT scary!
Keep reading.

This is NOT a scary story ... 5

"Mama, today by the bridge
Some human kids made me mad
They were afraid of me Mama
That made me feel sad."

"They said bats are all monsters
And that we should be feared
They said all bats were ugly
They said we were weird!"

"I'm not a monster
Those kids called me that
I'm not scary at all
I'm just a Little Boy Bat!"

"Some people get scared," said Mama.
"Especially of things in the dark
Perhaps you can help them
Let's talk tonight in the park."

7

When sunset arrived
The sky darkened from blue
Then from under the bridge
A million bats flew.

The tornado of bats whirled
And drew gasps from the crowd
Bats twirled high in the air
Filled the sky like a cloud.

LB was one bat in that swarm
He flew searching for treats
His goal was insects and moths
And tasty skeeters to eat.

The bats gobbled their supper
LB ate bugs by the dozens
He zoomed through the night
Played bat tag with his cousins.

Then Mama Bat flew in close
Pointed to trees down below
"Time to talk Little Boy Bat
There are things you
should know."

"Some humans are wrong about bats
Think we build nests in their hair
They say we're all blind and have rabies
They are taught to beware."

"What if I make them a book?" LB asked.
"Yes, that's what I can do
I'll tell them the facts
Explain things that aren't true!"

"I'll make a book about bats
Tell what I know of our kind
I'll write words and draw pictures
I'll leave it for them to find."

"That's a fabulous idea," said Mama. "I can help you if you like.

So will your dad.

Remember to ask your grandpa and grandma for help, too. They know lots about the history of our family and our kind."

Little Boy Bat went right to work. He thought about the mean things the human kids by the bridge had said about bats. He was determined to teach them some facts.

It's true, bats can fly
Which no other
mammal can do
Our wings are
our hands
Yes, we're
different
than you.

Bats are NOT blind
No, we surely are not
Bats have eyes just like you
But that's not all
that we've got.

From our mouth
and our nose
We make
high-pitched
sounds
The sounds
help bats 'see'
When we're flying around.

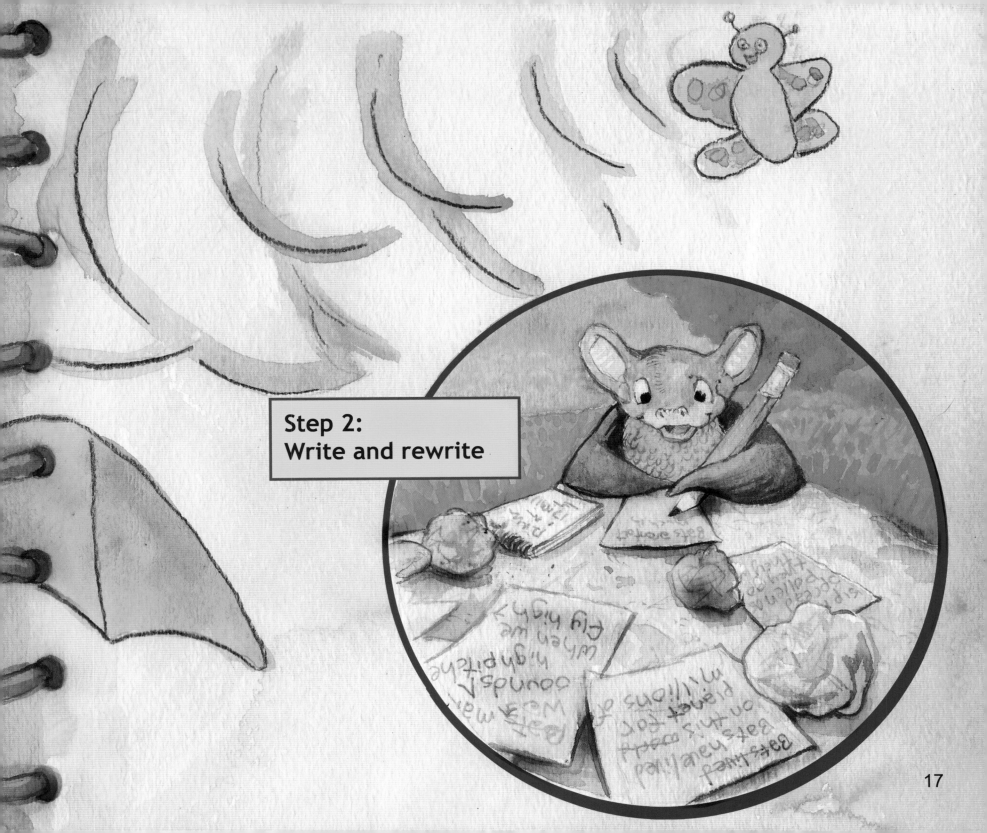

Step 2:
Write and rewrite

17

Bats aren't out much in daytime
We're not fond of the sun
We do our best work at night
We eat bugs by the ton.

Step 3:
Studies and drawings

Some bats sip nectar
Spread pollen as they go
Their work is important
They help other
plants grow.

Some bats do drink blood
Yes, that story is true
They bite animals and birds
They've no real interest in you!

Step 4:
Paint final artwork

Bats eat moths and mosquitoes
Some think fish are quite nice
Many bats eat fruit
Some big bats eat mice.

My Gramps is 14 years old
My, my, think of that
Not too old for a human
But real old for a bat.

Step 5:
Bind the book

How fast do
bats fly?
How big do
bats grow?
Go, do
some research
There's a
lot more to know!

Just one thing
to remember
As I finish this scrawl

Step 6:
Share!!!

Bats are NOT scary
No, we're NOT scary AT ALL!

Facts to drive you batty

Chiroptera is the scientific name for bats. It comes from two Greek words.

Cheir means hand.
Pteron means wing.

The largest known colony of free-tailed bats lives in Bracken Cave near San Antonio, Texas. The colony includes more than 15 million bats. That is almost twice the number of humans living in New York City.

300 Burgers

A single little brown bat can eat 60 moths or more than 1,000 small insects in one night. To eat like a bat, a 150-pound teenager would have to eat about 300 quarter-pound burgers in a single day.

Scientists say the fossil record shows that bats first appeared on Earth about 50-52 million years ago, during the Eocene epoch. Thunderbeasts, giant snakes and crocodiles, and lots of early mammals lived at that time.

Many types of bats living in the United States are in danger. A deadly illness is killing lots of bats. "White-Nose Syndrome" is caused by a fungus. Scientists are working to learn how to help bats.

Bat- 10,000'
Eiffel Tower- 986'
Great Pyramid- 455'
Statue of
Liberty- 305'

Mexican free-tailed bats are fast flyers. They are called the "jets" of the bat world. They can fly up to 10,000 feet in the air. They can zoom at a top speed of almost 60 miles per hour.

BAT POOP!!

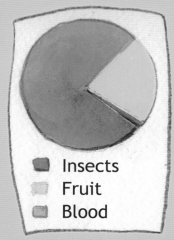

Bat poop is called guano. People use it as fertilizer to help grow crops. During the American Civil War, bat guano was used to make gunpowder.

About 70 percent of all bats living on Earth are insect eaters. The rest eat fruit. There are just a few kinds of vampire bats. They feed on the blood of cows, chickens, birds, and small animals.

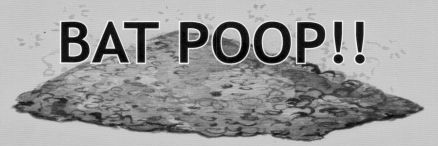

■ Insects
■ Fruit
■ Blood

Bats are NOT blind. Fruit eating bats have great vision. They use their eyes to find the fruit that they eat. Insect eating bats use a technique called echolocation to navigate and locate and catch their food, often while in flight. These bats open their mouth to call out ultra-high pitched sounds. Other bats shout the sounds through their nostrils. A bat's brain analyzes information from the returning echoes to "see" the environment around them. The sounds are much too high for the human ear to hear.

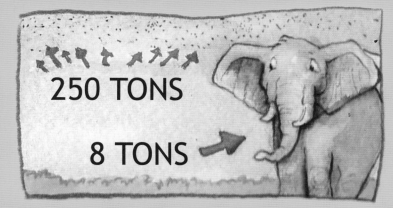

250 TONS

8 TONS

Colonies of free-tailed bats eat enormous amounts of insects. Some colonies include millions of bats. Those big colonies can consume tons of insects in a single night.

Researching Bats

BCI is dedicated to the enduring protection of the world's 1,300+ species of bats and their habitats and creating a world in which bats and humans successfully coexist.
http://www.batcon.org/

The Organization for Bat Conservation is a nonprofit environmental education organization dedicated to inspiring people to protect bats and to become good stewards of the environment. Its national 'Save the Bats' campaign gives kids and adults easy, meaningful ways to get involved in conservation.
http://www.batconservation.org/

Start by thinking about what you already know or think you know about bats.
Do you have any questions? Write them down. Then go looking for answers.
Be open to new information. Keep track of what you find out. Personalize it - write a story!! Doing something creative with your findings can help you remember and add life to the information.

Ask your parents, relatives and friends what they know.

Visit your local and school library.

Some other web sites to explore:

Defenders of Wildlife
http://www.defenders.org/bats/bats

Encyclopedia Smithsonian – Bat facts
http://www.si.edu/Encyclopedia_SI/nmnh/batfacts.htm

Kartchner Caverns State Park -- Benson, Arizona
http://azstateparks.com/Parks/KACA/

Carlsbad Caverns National Park – Bat Flight Program
http://www.nps.gov/cave/planyourvisit/bat_flight_program.htm

How to Help Bats

Educate

You've already started helping bats by reading this book and learning about bats.

What's the first thing I told you?

BATS ARE NOT SCARY!

Spread the word! Tell others what you have learned.

SAVE THE BATS

Be a Friend to Bats
http://www.savebats.org

Build a Bat House

A bat house is easy to make in an afternoon. Its shallow construction is designed specifically to attract bats, which like cramped, dark spaces for nesting. Kids can do lots of the work involved in making this bat house, including measuring, driving screws, and painting. Parents need to help out with the sawing. Once you've finished it, hang your bat house high in a sunny corner of your backyard, and the bats will soon find a stylish new home.
Find plans at: http://www.batcon.org/bathouse

Grow Bat Friendly Plants

Bats feed at night. Planting night-blooming flowers will attract night bugs which will attract bats. Bats also like water features like ponds and birdbaths where insects might gather.

Donate

Bats play very important roles in many of the Earth's ecosystems. Learn more about how you can help bats at: http://www.supportbats.org

Join together

Join your local bat group and go on local bat walks.

Narrator and budding young author

Name: Little Boy Bat. A medium-size bat. His nickname is L.B.

Species: Mexican free-tailed bat (*Tadarida brasiliensis*).

Home: L.B. lives in a colony with more than a million of his friends and cousins. They roost together under the Congress Avenue Bridge over the Colorado River in downtown Austin, Texas.

Size: Weighs only 0.4 to 0.5 ounces (11-14 grams). Wingspan is 12 to 14 inches (30-35 centimeters).

Color: Fur is dark brown to gray. Broad ears are brown or gray.

Beauty marks: Ears point forward. Lips are wrinkled. Long, narrow wings.

Diet: Small insects and moths, many of which are crop pests. Does NOT like pizza, tacos, hot dogs or French fries.

Life Span: Lives up to 11 years in the wild.

Habitat: Likes to roost in caves. But will also live in attics, old buildings, or under bridges. Likes to live near water which attracts lots of tasty insect food.

Range: Lives across lower half of the United States and Mexico. Found south throughout most of Central America and into South America.

Creating a Children's Book

What Conrad does

I am always looking for ideas. I watch. I listen. Ideas are everywhere. Once I grab onto an idea I hold on as tight as I can.

The goal is to turn that idea into a fun story that I can share with readers everywhere. But making scientific facts fun to read about is a challenge. I try to use storytelling techniques to grab my readers by the eyes. I work hard to get my audience to read Page 1. The challenge is to make them want to turn the page and keep reading the rest of the story. Once I have an idea I start my research. I hit the library, and I hit it hard. I visit in person or on line. I find as many reference sources as I can related to my subject matter. I also interview scientists or experts on the topic of my book. I want my books to be fun, but I want them to be factual and as accurate as possible. Good science writing is really story telling at a different level. I fill my brain and notebooks with facts and information.

Now the real fun begins. I begin to write on my computer. I write, and write, and then I write some more. Sometimes I write five, six, 10 or 15 drafts of a story before I am satisfied. The best writers are really good "rewriters." Writing about science and nature requires a knack for word choice and explanation. Done well, the best writing will always pique the reader's curiosity to learn more, regardless of their age. I've done my job well if I can make a reader curious to learn more.

What Nate does

The first step I take is I read the story over and over again and start to imagine pictures that the words inspire.

Then, I gather reference photos. I study and make drawings of the animal the book is about.

Next, I make a dummy book. I tape together the number of pages the book is to be. I cut apart the words and begin taping them in this book trying to spread them evenly throughout.

I make quick pencil drawings in the dummy book of my ideas for the pictures that will illustrate what is being expressed with the words. I may make several dummy books looking for the best ideas.

I redraw in pencil the best ideas with greater detail and show them to the editor or publisher.

Approved pictures are then painted and the finished artwork is then sent to be photographed and put in the book.

You can watch a video about the making of "Big Horns Don't Honk" in the school visit section of my website at www.natepjensen.com

How to Draw a Bat

Start simple. Draw a circle with a triangle on both sides. Put this on top of an oval. Then draw a big triangle behind the oval.

Can you draw an oval, a circle, rectangles, and triangles? Yes? Then you can draw a bat.

Add some rectangles coming out of the oval. Add a circle to the end of each. Add some half circles to the big circle.

Turn the circles into hands with some extra lines. Add circles in the half circles for the eyes. Make rows of squiggles in the oval for the hair. Make lines and bumps in the big triangle for the classic bat wing shape.

You can draw anything if you look for and find the basic shapes in things. Try it! Look around you. What shapes do you see?